Whoopie Pies & Cake Pops

Published by Top That! Publishing plc
Tide Mill Way, Woodbridge, Suffolk, IP12 IAP, UK
www.topthatpublishing.com
Copyright © 2013 Top That! Publishing plc
All rights reserved
0 2 4 6 8 9 7 5 3 1
Printed and bound in China

Contents

Whoopie Pies

Cake Pops

The Author

Dominique Godfrey has been baking and making delicious whoopie pies and cake pops for the last three years. Her business, Sugarplum Cupcakes based in East Anglia, UK, hosts a whole range of sugarcraft workshops for all ages and abilities including cupcakes, cake pops and mini cakes. For more information visit, www.sugarplumcupcakes.co.uk

Cooking Equipment

Before you begin to get creative in the kitchen, it's a good idea to take a look through the drawers and cupboards to make sure you know where all the cooking equipment is kept.

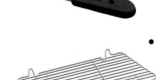

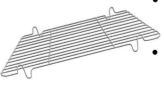

- To complete the recipes in this book, you will need to use a selection of everyday cooking equipment and utensils, such as mixing bowls, saucepans, a sieve, a wire rack and a cutting board.

- Of course, you'll need to weigh and measure the ingredients, so you'll need measuring cups and spoons too.

- Some of the recipes tell you to use a whisk. Ask an adult to help you use an electric mixer, or you can use a whisk yourself—you'll just have to work extra hard!

- To make some of the whoopie pies and cake pops, you'll need to use some special equipment. These items (and others that you may not have to hand) are listed at the start of each recipe.

- To make the whoopie pies, it is best to use special whoopie pie pans which can easily be bought from kitchen stores.

- The measurements given in this book are approximate. Use the same measurement conversions throughout your recipe (cups or ounces) to maintain the correct ratios.

⚠️ Safety & Hygiene

It is important to take care in the kitchen as there are lots of potential hazards and hygiene risks.

- Take Note! Adult supervision is required for all the recipes in this book.

- Before starting any cooking always wash your hands.

- Cover any cuts with a bandage.

- Wear an apron to protect your clothes.

- Always make sure that all the equipment you use is clean.

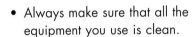

- If you need to use a sharp knife to cut up something hard, ask an adult to help you. Always use a cutting board.

- Remember that pans in the oven and on the cooktop can get very hot. Always ask an adult to turn on the oven and to get things in and out of the oven for you.

- Always ask an adult for help if you are using anything electrical —like an electric mixer.

- Be careful when heating anything in a pan on top of the cooktop. Keep the handle turned inwards to avoid accidentally knocking the pan.

- Keep your pets out of the kitchen while cooking.

Getting Started

Making your own whoopie pies and cake pops is great fun and really quite easy. Best of all, everyone will enjoy what you create!

Measuring:

Use measuring cups or spoons to measure exactly how much of each ingredient you need.

Mixing:

Use a spoon, whisk or electric mixer to mix the ingredients together.

Equipment:

To make all the whoopies pies in this book you will need two whoopie pie pans.

Making the cake pops in this book will require some special equipment. See pages 71–72.

Always ask an adult for help if you are not sure about anything.

Read through each recipe to make sure you've got all the equipment and ingredients you need before you start.

Creating recipes:

Once you've made a recipe in this book a few times, think about whether you could make your own version. Try mixing and matching the whoopie pie fillings or think of your own awesome cake pop designs. Try to think up names for the things you create!

Whoopie Pies

Introduction

Whoopie pies are a delicious sweet treat that originated from the north east of America and are best described as a mixture between a cookie and a cake sandwiched together with a scrumptious sweet filling.

Easy to bake, with an endless choice of flavors and fillings, whoopie pies are the ideal treat to prepare, bake and enjoy.

Follow these simple step-by-step recipes and discover the delights of making whoopie pies!

Whoopie Pie Equipment

To make the whoopie pies in this book, you may find it easier to use special whoopie pie pans. These have shallow, round holes to make sure the whoopie pies come out looking perfect. Whoopie pie pans can be found in some supermarkets, baking stores or online. If you haven't got whoopie pie pans, simply pipe or spoon the cake mixture onto a baking sheet, trying to keep the mixture as round-shaped as possible.

Blueberry Whoopie Pies
with Lime Cream Cheese Filling

Blueberry Whoopie Pies

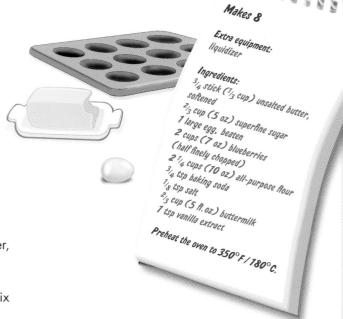

Makes 8

Extra equipment:
liquidizer

Ingredients:
3/4 stick (1/3 cup) unsalted butter, softened
2/3 cup (5 oz) superfine sugar
1 large egg, beaten
2 cups (7 oz) blueberries (half finely chopped)
2 1/4 cups (10 oz) all-purpose flour
3/4 tsp baking soda
1/8 tsp salt
2/3 cup (5 fl. oz) buttermilk
1 tsp vanilla extract

Preheat the oven to 350°F / 180°C.

1 Grease the whoopie pie pans with a little butter.

2 Cream the softened butter and sugar together in a bowl until light and fluffy, then gradually add the beaten egg.

3 Process half of the blueberries in a liquidizer for several minutes until they have broken down into a liquid or very small pieces. If you don't have a liquidizer, use an electric mixer.

4 Add to the creamed butter mixture and mix well for a few minutes.

5 Sift the flour, baking soda and salt together in another bowl.

6 Gradually add a third of the dry ingredients to the butter mixture, followed by a third of the buttermilk. Continue adding both alternately and then add the vanilla extract. Mix well until all of the ingredients are combined to form a thick, smooth cake mixture.

7 Fill a piping bag or use a tablespoon to transfer the cake mixture evenly onto the whoopie pie pans.

8 Place the remaining blueberries onto the pies, pushing them into the cake mixture.

9 Bake in the oven for 12–14 minutes, until risen and firm to the touch.

10 Cool for 5 minutes in the pans before transferring to a wire rack to cool completely.

Lime Cream Cheese Filling

1 Beat the butter and confectioner's sugar together for a few minutes using a whisk or an electric mixer until well mixed.

2 Add the cream cheese and beat together until the filling is light and fluffy.

3 Finally, add the lime juice and zest and mix well.

4 Using either a piping bag or a spoon, spread the filling evenly over one half of the whoopie pie and sandwich together with the second half.

Ingredients:
1/2 stick (1/4 cup) unsalted butter
2 1/4 cups (10 1/2 oz) confectioner's sugar
1/2 cup (4 1/2 oz) cream cheese
2 tbsps fresh lime juice
1 tbsp lime zest, finely grated

Carrot & Raisin Whoopie Pies
with Cream Cheese Filling

Carrot & Raisin Whoopie Pies

1 Grease the whoopie pie pans with a little butter.

2 Cream the softened butter and sugar together in a bowl until light and fluffy, then gradually add the beaten egg and vanilla extract and mix well.

3 Sift in half of the flour, the ginger, cinnamon, nutmeg, baking soda and salt, followed by half of the buttermilk and mix well. Then add the rest of the ingredients and mix until combined to form a thick, smooth cake mixture.

4 Add the grated carrot and raisins and stir until evenly combined.

5 Fill a piping bag or use a tablespoon to transfer the cake mixture evenly onto the whoopie pie pans.

6 Bake in the oven for 12–14 minutes, until risen and firm to the touch.

7 Cool for 5 minutes in the pans before transferring to a wire rack to cool completely.

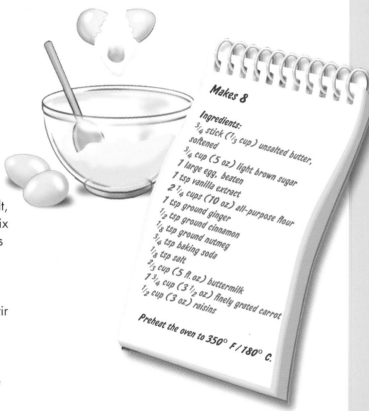

Makes 8

Ingredients:
3/4 stick (1/3 cup) unsalted butter, softened
3/4 cup (5 oz) light brown sugar
1 large egg, beaten
1 tsp vanilla extract
2 1/4 cups (10 oz) all-purpose flour
1 tsp ground ginger
1/2 tsp ground cinnamon
1/8 tsp ground nutmeg
3/4 tsp baking soda
1/8 tsp salt
2/3 cup (5 fl. oz) buttermilk
1 3/4 cup (3 1/2 oz) finely grated carrot
1/2 cup (3 oz) raisins

Preheat the oven to 350° F / 180° C.

Cream Cheese Filling

Ingredients:
1/2 stick (1/4 cup) unsalted butter
2 1/4 cups (10 1/2 oz) confectioner's sugar
1/2 cup (4 1/2 oz) cream cheese

1 Beat the butter and confectioner's sugar together for a few minutes using a whisk or an electric mixer until well mixed.

2 Add the cream cheese and beat together until the filling is light and fluffy.

3 Using either a piping bag or a spoon, spread the filling evenly over one half of the whoopie pie and sandwich together with the second half.

Chocolate & Banana Whoopie Pies
with Chocolate Buttercream

Chocolate & Banana Whoopie Pies

1 Grease the whoopie pie pans with a little butter.

2 Cream the softened butter and sugar together in a bowl until light and fluffy, then add the beaten egg.

3 Sift the flour, baking cocoa, baking soda and salt together in another bowl.

4 Gradually add a third of the dry ingredients to the mixture, followed by a third of the buttermilk. Continue adding both alternately and mix well until all of the ingredients are combined to form a thick, smooth cake mixture.

5 Mash two overripe bananas in a bowl and add to the cake mixture, stirring well.

6 Fill a piping bag or use a tablespoon to transfer the cake mixture evenly onto the whoopie pie pans. Bake in the oven for 12–14 minutes until risen and firm to the touch.

7 Cool for 5 minutes in the pans before transferring to a wire rack to cool completely.

Makes 8

Ingredients:
3/4 stick (1/3 cup) unsalted butter, softened
2/3 cup (5 oz) dark brown sugar
1 large egg, beaten
2 1/4 cups (10 oz) all-purpose flour
1/3 cup (1 1/2 oz) baking cocoa
2 1/2 tsps baking soda
1/8 tsp salt
3/4 cup (6 fl. oz) buttermilk
2 overripe bananas

Preheat the oven to 350°F / 180°C.

Chocolate Buttercream

Ingredients:
4 ¾ cups (1 lb 5 oz) confectioner's sugar
¾ cup (3 oz) baking cocoa
1 ¾ sticks (⅞ cup) unsalted butter
5 tbsps milk
chocolate sprinkles, to decorate

1 Mix the confectioner's sugar, baking cocoa and butter together for a few minutes using a whisk or an electric mixer.

2 Slowly add the milk and continue mixing for 5 minutes until the buttercream is light and fluffy.

3 Using either a piping bag or a spoon, spread the buttercream evenly over one half of the whoopie pie and sandwich together with the second half.

4 Place chocolate sprinkles around the edge of the whoopie pie to decorate.

Top Tip!
Assembled whoopie pies can be frozen for up to a month—so you always have a secret stash!

Chocolate Chip Whoopie Pies
with Vanilla Buttercream

Chocolate Chip Whoopie Pies

Makes 8

Ingredients:
3/4 stick (1/3 cup) unsalted butter, softened
2/3 cup (5 oz) superfine sugar
1 large egg, beaten
1 tsp vanilla extract
2 1/4 cups (10 oz) all-purpose flour
3/4 tsp baking soda
1/8 tsp salt
2/3 cup (5 fl. oz) buttermilk
1/2 cup (3 1/2 oz) chocolate chips

Preheat the oven to 350°F / 180°C.

1 Grease the whoopie pie pans with a little butter.

2 Cream the softened butter and sugar together in a bowl until light and fluffy, then gradually add the beaten egg and vanilla extract.

3 Sift the flour, baking soda and salt together in another bowl.

4 Gradually add a third of the dry ingredients to the mixture, followed by a third of the buttermilk. Continue adding both alternately and mix well until just before you add the last amount of dry ingredients.

5 Stir in the chocolate chips and then add the remaining flour to form a thick, smooth cake mixture.

6 Fill a piping bag or use a tablespoon to transfer the cake mixture evenly onto the whoopie pie pans.

7 Bake in the oven for 12–14 minutes until risen and firm to the touch.

8 Cool for 5 minutes in the pans before transferring to a wire rack to cool completely.

Vanilla Buttercream

Ingredients:
4 cups (1 lb 1 oz) confectioner's sugar
1 ¼ sticks (²/₃ cup) unsalted butter
3 tbsps milk
½ tsp vanilla extract

1 Beat the confectioner's sugar and butter together for a few minutes using a whisk or an electric mixer until well mixed.

2 Add the milk and vanilla extract and beat together until the buttercream is light and fluffy.

3 Using either a piping bag or a spoon, spread the buttercream evenly over one half of the whoopie pie and sandwich together with the second half.

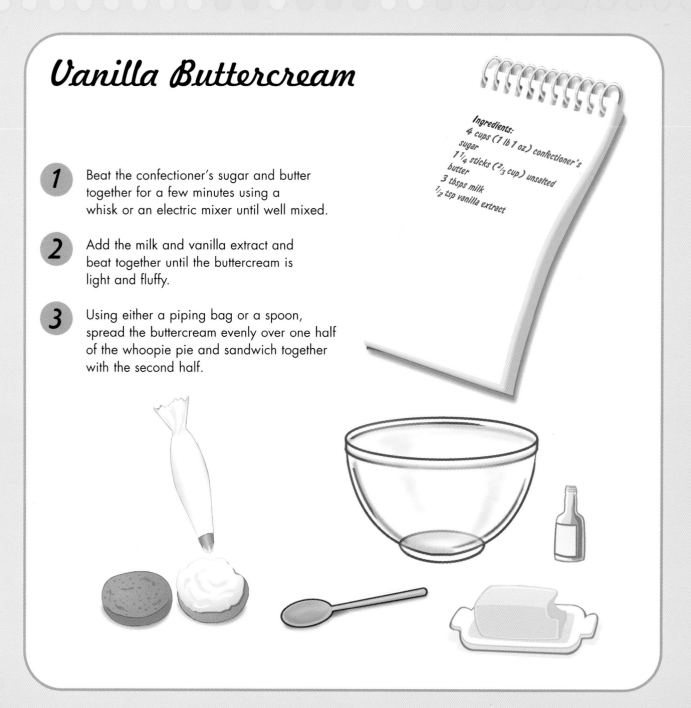

Chocolate Orange Whoopie Pies
with Orange Buttercream

Chocolate Orange Whoopie Pies

1 Grease the whoopie pie pans with a little butter.

2 Cream the softened butter and sugar together in a bowl until light and fluffy, then gradually add the beaten egg until well mixed.

3 Add the grated zest and juice from an orange and mix well.

4 Sift the flour, baking cocoa, baking soda and salt together into another bowl.

5 Gradually add a third of the dry ingredients to the mixture, followed by a third of the buttermilk. Continue adding both alternately and mix well until all of the ingredients are combined to form a thick, smooth cake mixture.

6 Fill a piping bag or use a tablespoon to transfer the cake mixture evenly onto the whoopie pie pans.

7 Bake in the oven for 12–14 minutes until risen and firm to the touch.

8 Cool for 5 minutes in the pans before transferring to a wire rack to cool completely.

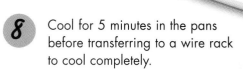

Makes 8

Ingredients:
¾ stick (⅓ cup) unsalted butter, softened
¾ cup (5 oz) dark brown sugar
1 large egg, beaten
1 tbsp finely grated orange zest
4 tbsps fresh orange juice
2 ¼ cups (10 oz) all-purpose flour
⅓ cup (1 ½ oz) baking cocoa
1 ½ tsps baking soda
⅛ tsp salt
⅔ cup (5 fl. oz) buttermilk

Orange Buttercream

Ingredients:
1 ¼ sticks (⅔ cup) unsalted butter
4 cups (1 lb 1 oz) confectioner's sugar
3 tbsps milk
½ tsp orange extract
a drop of orange food coloring

1. Beat the butter and confectioner's sugar together for a few minutes using a whisk or an electric mixer until well mixed.

2. Add the milk and orange extract, mixing well for several minutes until the buttercream is light and fluffy.

3. Finally, add a drop or two of orange food coloring and mix again until the color is evenly combined.

4. Using either a piping bag or a spoon, spread the buttercream evenly over half of the whoopie pies and sandwich together with the second half.

Top Tip!
This is a great recipe for Halloween—try adding a spooky face onto the top of each whoopie pie with orange frosting.

Chocolate & Peppermint Whoopie Pies
with Peppermint Buttercream

Chocolate & Peppermint Whoopie Pies

1. Grease the whoopie pie pans with a little butter.

2. Cream the softened butter and sugar together in a bowl until light and fluffy, then gradually add the beaten egg and peppermint extract until well mixed.

3. Sift the flour, baking cocoa, baking soda and salt together into another bowl.

4. Gradually add a third of the dry ingredients to the mixture, followed by a third of the buttermilk. Continue adding both alternately and mix well until all of the ingredients are combined to form a thick, smooth cake mixture.

5. Fill a piping bag or use a tablespoon to transfer the cake mixture evenly onto the whoopie pie pans.

6. Bake in the oven for 12–14 minutes until risen and firm to the touch.

7. Cool for 5 minutes in the pans before transferring to a wire rack to cool completely.

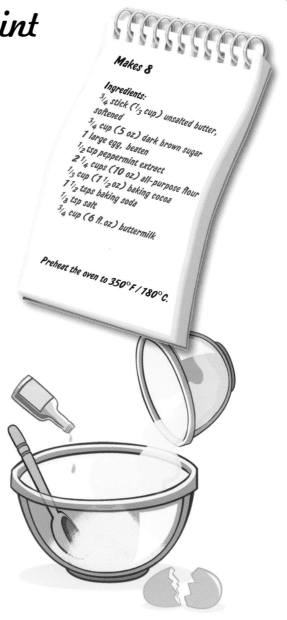

Makes 8

Ingredients:
3/4 stick (1/3 cup) unsalted butter, softened
3/4 cup (5 oz) dark brown sugar
1 large egg, beaten
1/2 tsp peppermint extract
2 1/4 cups (10 oz) all-purpose flour
1/3 cup (1 1/2 oz) baking cocoa
1 1/2 tsps baking soda
1/8 tsp salt
3/4 cup (6 fl. oz) buttermilk

Preheat the oven to 350°F / 180°C.

Peppermint Buttercream

1 Beat the butter and confectioner's sugar together for a few minutes using a whisk or an electric mixer until well mixed.

2 Gradually add the milk and peppermint extract, mixing well for several minutes until the buttercream is light and fluffy.

3 Using either a piping bag or a spoon, spread the buttercream evenly onto half of the whoopie pies, sandwiching the remaining pies on top.

4 Roll the edges of each whoopie pie in the crushed candy canes to decorate.

Ingredients:
1 1/4 sticks (2/3 cup) unsalted butter
4 cups (1 lb 1 oz) confectioner's sugar
2 tbsps milk
1/2 tsp peppermint extract
1/2 cup (3 oz) crushed candy canes (approx. 6 canes)

Coconut
Whoopie Pies
with Coconut Cream

Coconut Whoopie Pies

1. Grease the whoopie pie pans with a little butter.

2. Cream the softened butter and sugar together in a bowl until light and fluffy, then gradually add the beaten egg and coconut extract.

3. Sift the flour, shredded coconut, baking soda and salt together in another bowl.

4. Gradually add half of the dry sifted ingredients, followed by half of the coconut milk and then repeat until all of the ingredients are combined to form a thick, smooth cake mixture.

5. Fill a piping bag or use a tablespoon to transfer the cake mixture evenly onto the whoopie pie pans.

6. Bake in the oven for 12–14 minutes until risen and firm to the touch.

7. Cool for 5 minutes in the pans before transferring to a wire rack to cool completely.

Makes 8

Ingredients:
3/4 stick (1/3 cup) unsalted butter, softened
2/3 cup (5 oz) superfine sugar
1 large egg, beaten
1 tsp coconut extract
2 1/4 cups (10 oz) all-purpose flour
2/3 cup (2 oz) shredded coconut
3/4 tsp baking soda
1/8 tsp salt
2/3 cup (5 fl. oz) coconut milk

Preheat the oven to 350°F/180°C.

Coconut Cream

1 Beat the butter and confectioner's sugar together for a few minutes using a whisk or an electric mixer until well mixed.

2 Add the coconut milk and shredded coconut and mix together for several minutes until the buttercream is light and fluffy.

3 Using either a piping bag or a spoon, spread the buttercream evenly over one half of the whoopie pie and sandwich together with the second half.

4 Sprinkle extra shredded coconut around the edge of the whoopie pie to decorate.

Ingredients:
¾ stick (⅓ cup) unsalted butter
2 cups (9 oz) confectioner's sugar
2 tbsps coconut milk
2 tbsps shredded coconut
(plus extra for decoration)

Dipped Double Chocolate Whoopie Pies
with Chocolate Buttercream

Dipped Double Chocolate Whoopie Pies

1 Grease the whoopie pie pans with a little butter.

2 Cream the softened butter and sugar together in a bowl until light and fluffy, then gradually add the beaten egg and vanilla extract until well mixed.

3 Sift the flour, baking cocoa, baking soda and salt together into another bowl.

4 Gradually add a third of the dry ingredients to the mixture, followed by a third of the buttermilk. Continue adding both alternately and mix well until all of the ingredients are combined to form a thick, smooth cake mixture.

5 Fill a piping bag or use a tablespoon to transfer the cake mixture evenly onto the whoopie pie pans.

6 Bake in the oven for 12–14 minutes until risen and firm to the touch.

7 Cool for 5 minutes in the pans before transferring to a wire rack to cool completely.

Makes 2 batches
Great dough!

Makes 8

Ingredients:
3/4 stick (1/3 cup) unsalted butter, softened
3/4 cup (5 oz) dark brown sugar
1 large egg, beaten
1 tsp vanilla extract
2 1/4 cups (10 oz) all-purpose flour
1/3 cup (1 1/2 oz) baking cocoa
1 1/2 tsps baking soda
1/8 tsp salt
3/4 cup (6 fl. oz) buttermilk

Preheat the oven to 350°F / 180°C.

Chocolate Buttercream

Extra equipment:
cooling tray
baking parchment paper

Ingredients:
1 ³/₄ sticks (⁷/₈ cup) unsalted butter
4 ³/₄ cups (1 lb 5 oz) confectioner's sugar
²/₃ cup (3 oz) baking cocoa
5 tbsps milk
5 oz bittersweet chocolate

1 Beat the butter, confectioner's sugar and baking cocoa together for a few minutes using a whisk or an electric mixer until well mixed.

2 Gradually add the milk, mixing well for several minutes until the buttercream is light and fluffy.

3 Using either a piping bag or a spoon, spread the buttercream evenly onto half of the whoopie pies, sandwiching the remaining pies on top.

4 Carefully melt the chocolate in a microwave stirring at 30 second intervals, or melt the chocolate in a bowl over a saucepan of simmering water, making sure the bowl doesn't touch the water.

5 Carefully dip half of each whoopie pie into the melted chocolate, then place carefully on a cooling tray to set. Put baking parchment paper underneath the tray to catch any excess dripping chocolate.

Top Tip!
For a quick and easy alternative filling, try using chocolate and hazelnut spread.

Gingerbread Whoopie Pies
with Lemon Buttercream

Gingerbread Whoopie Pies

1. Grease the whoopie pie pans with a little butter.

2. Cream the softened butter and sugar together in a bowl until light and fluffy, then gradually add the beaten egg and molasses and mix well.

3. Sift in half of the flour, ginger, cinnamon, nutmeg, cloves, baking soda and salt, followed by half of the buttermilk. Repeat until all of the ingredients are combined to form a thick, smooth cake mixture.

4. Fill a piping bag or use a tablespoon to transfer the cake mixture evenly onto the whoopie pie pans.

5. Bake in the oven for 12–14 minutes until risen and firm to the touch.

6. Cool for 5 minutes in the pans before transferring to a wire rack to cool completely.

Makes 8

Ingredients:
3/4 stick (1/3 cup) unsalted butter, softened
3/4 cup (5 oz) brown sugar
1 large egg, beaten
1 tbsp molasses
2 1/4 cups (10 oz) all-purpose flour
1 1/2 tsps ground ginger
1/2 tsp ground cinnamon
1/8 tsp ground nutmeg
1/8 tsp ground cloves
3/4 tsp baking soda
1/8 tsp salt
2/3 cup (5 fl. oz) buttermilk

Preheat the oven to 350°F/180°C.

Lemon Buttercream

1 Beat the confectioner's sugar and butter together for a few minutes using a whisk or an electric mixer until well mixed.

2 Add the milk, lemon juice and zest and mix for 5 minutes until the buttercream is light and fluffy.

3 Using either a piping bag or a spoon, spread the buttercream evenly over one half of the whoopie pie and sandwich together with the second half.

Ingredients:
4 cups (1 lb 1 oz) confectioner's sugar
1 ¼ sticks (²/₃ cup) unsalted butter
2 tbsps milk
2 tbsps fresh lemon juice
2 tsps lemon zest, finely grated
lemon curd (optional)

Top Tip!
For an extra lemony twist, spread lemon curd over the top of the whoopie pie and sprinkle with a little lemon zest.

Lemon
Whoopie Pies
with Lemon Cream Cheese Filling

Lemon Whoopie Pies

1. Grease the whoopie pie pans with a little butter.

2. Cream the softened butter and sugar together in a bowl until light and fluffy, then gradually add the beaten egg, lemon juice and finely grated lemon zest.

3. Sift the flour, baking soda and salt together in another bowl.

4. Gradually add a third of the dry ingredients to the mixture, followed by a third of the buttermilk. Continue adding both alternately and mix well until all of the ingredients are combined to form a thick, smooth cake mixture.

5. Fill a piping bag or use a tablespoon to transfer the cake mixture evenly onto the whoopie pie pans.

6. Bake in the oven for 12–14 minutes until risen and firm to the touch.

7. Cool for 5 minutes in the pans before transferring to a wire rack to cool completely.

Good for one Batch • a few more lemon
Don't fill pans so much
(Dough too sticky – more flour)

Makes 8

Ingredients:
3/4 stick (1/3 cup) unsalted butter, softened
2/3 cup (5 oz) superfine sugar
1 large egg, beaten
2 tbsps fresh lemon juice
2 tsps lemon zest, finely grated
2 1/4 cups (10 oz) all-purpose flour
3/4 tsp baking soda
1/8 tsp salt
2/3 cup (5 fl. oz) buttermilk

Preheat the oven to 350° F / 180° C.

Lemon Cream Cheese Filling

Ingredients:
½ stick (¼ cup) unsalted butter
2 ½ cups (10 ½ oz) confectioner's sugar
½ cup (4 ½ oz) cream cheese
2 tbsps fresh lemon juice

1 Beat the butter and confectioner's sugar together for a few minutes using a whisk or an electric mixer until well mixed.

2 Add the cream cheese and beat together until the filling is light and fluffy.

3 Finally, add the lemon juice and mix well.

4 Using either a piping bag or a spoon, spread the filling evenly over one half of the whoopie pie and sandwich together with the second half.

Oatmeal Whoopie Pies
with Maple Buttercream

Oatmeal Whoopie Pies

1 Grease the whoopie pie pans with a little butter.

2 Cream the softened butter and sugar together in a bowl until light and fluffy, then gradually add the beaten egg and mix well.

3 Sift the flour, baking soda, baking powder, cinnamon and salt together in another bowl.

4 Gradually add the dry ingredients to the butter mixture, along with the boiling water. Mix well and then stir in the oats.

5 Fill a piping bag or use a tablespoon to transfer the cake mixture evenly onto the whoopie pie pans.

6 Bake in the oven for 12–14 minutes until risen and firm to the touch.

7 Cool for 5 minutes in the pans before transferring to a wire rack to cool completely.

Makes 8

Ingredients:
3/4 stick (1/3 cup) unsalted butter, softened
3/4 cup (5 oz) light brown sugar
1 large egg, beaten
2 cups (9 oz) all-purpose flour
1/2 tsp baking soda
1/2 tsp baking powder
1/2 tsp ground cinnamon
1/8 tsp salt
4 1/2 tbsps boiling water
1 cup (3 oz) rolled oats

Preheat the oven to 350°F / 180°C.

Maple Buttercream

Ingredients:
1 ½ sticks (¾ cup) unsalted butter
4 cups (1 lb 1 oz) confectioner's sugar
3 tbsps maple syrup
2 tbsps milk
½ cup chopped pecan nuts

1 Beat the butter and confectioner's sugar together for a few minutes using a whisk or an electric mixer until well mixed.

2 Add the maple syrup and milk and mix for several minutes until the buttercream is light and fluffy.

3 Using a spoon, spread the buttercream evenly over one half of the whoopie pie and sandwich together with the second half.

4 Sprinkle chopped pecan nuts around the edge of the whoopie pie to decorate.

Oreo Cookies & Cream Whoopie Pies
with Cookie Buttercream

Oreo Cookies & Cream Whoopie Pies

1 Grease the whoopie pie pans with a little butter.

2 Cream the softened butter and sugar together in a bowl until light and fluffy, then gradually add the beaten egg until well mixed.

3 Melt the chocolate in the microwave, stirring at 30 second intervals, being careful not to burn it.

4 Process the cookies in a liquidizer until they have a crumb-like consistency. If you haven't got a liquidizer, ask an adult to use an electric mixer.

5 Combine the melted chocolate with the cookie crumbs and add, with the vanilla extract, to the cake mixture.

6 Sift the flour, baking soda and salt together into another bowl.

7 Gradually add a third of the dry ingredients to the mixture, followed by a third of the buttermilk. Continue adding both alternately and mix well until all of the ingredients are combined to form a thick, smooth cake mix.

8 Fill a piping bag or use a tablespoon to transfer the cake mixture evenly onto the whoopie pie pans.

9 Bake in the oven for 12–14 minutes until risen and firm to the touch.

10 Cool for 5 minutes in the pan before transferring to a wire rack to cool completely.

Makes 8

Extra equipment:
liquidizer

Ingredients:
3/4 stick (1/3 cup) unsalted butter, softened
3/4 cup (5 oz) dark brown sugar
1 large egg, beaten
3 1/2 oz bittersweet chocolate
9 (3 1/2 oz) vanilla-filled (Oreo) chocolate cookies, crumbled
1 tsp vanilla extract
2 1/4 cups (10 oz) all-purpose flour
1 1/2 tsps baking soda
1/8 tsp salt
2/3 cup (5 fl. oz) buttermilk

Preheat the oven to 350°F / 180°C.

Cookie Buttercream

Ingredients:
1 ½ sticks (¾ cup) unsalted butter
4 cups (1 lb 1 oz) confectioner's sugar
2 tbsps milk
½ tsp vanilla extract
9 (3 ½ oz) vanilla-filled (Oreo) chocolate cookies

1 Beat the butter and confectioner's sugar together for a few minutes using a whisk or an electric mixer until well mixed.

2 Add the milk and vanilla extract, mixing well for several minutes until the buttercream is light and fluffy.

3 Roughly chop the cookies into small pieces and add to the buttercream.

4 Using a spoon, spread the buttercream evenly over one half of the whoopie pie and sandwich together with the second half.

Top Tip!
Create your own favorite whoopie "cookie" pie by using any of your favorite cookies!

Peanut Butter Whoopie Pies
with Chocolate & Hazelnut Buttercream

Peanut Butter Whoopie Pies

1 Grease the whoopie pie pans with a little butter.

2 Cream the softened butter and sugar together in a bowl until light and fluffy, then gradually add the beaten egg, vanilla extract and peanut butter.

3 Sift the flour, baking soda and salt together in another bowl.

4 Gradually add a third of the dry ingredients to the mixture, followed by a third of the buttermilk. Continue adding both alternately and mix well until all of the ingredients are combined to form a thick, smooth cake mixture.

5 Fill a piping bag or use a tablespoon to transfer the cake mixture evenly onto the whoopie pie pans.

6 Bake in the oven for 12–14 minutes until risen and firm to the touch.

7 Cool for 5 minutes in the pans before transferring to a wire rack to cool completely.

Makes 8

Ingredients:
¾ stick (⅓ cup) unsalted butter, softened
⅔ cup (5 oz) superfine sugar
1 large egg, beaten
1 tsp vanilla extract
⅓ cup (3 oz) peanut butter
2¼ cups (10 oz) all-purpose flour
¾ tsp baking soda
⅛ tsp salt
⅔ cup (5 fl. oz) buttermilk

Preheat the oven to 350°F / 180°C.

Chocolate & Hazelnut Buttercream

1 Beat the butter for a few minutes using a whisk or an electric mixer until smooth.

2 Add the chocolate and hazelnut spread and mix again until combined.

3 Add the confectioner's sugar, a little at a time, until well mixed.

4 Finally, add the milk and mix until you have a smooth consistency.

5 Using a spoon, spread the buttercream evenly over one half of the whoopie pie and sandwich together with the second half.

Ingredients:
1 stick (1/2 cup) unsalted butter
1 cup (10 1/2 oz) chocolate and hazelnut spread
1 cup (4 1/2 oz) confectioner's sugar
2 tbsps milk

Top Tip!
Add chocolate chips to this whoopie pie recipe for a double chocolate hit!

Rainbow
Whoopie Pies
with Rainbow Buttercream

Rainbow Whoopie Pies

Makes 8

Extra equipment:
5 piping bags

Ingredients:
¾ stick (⅓ cup) unsalted butter, softened
⅔ cup (5 oz) superfine sugar
1 large egg, beaten
1 tsp vanilla extract
2¼ cups (10 oz) all-purpose flour
¾ tsp baking soda
⅛ tsp salt
⅔ cup (5 fl. oz) buttermilk
5 food colorings, any colors

Preheat the oven to 350°F / 180°C.

1 Grease the whoopie pie pans with a little butter.

2 Cream the softened butter and sugar together in a bowl until light and fluffy, then gradually add the beaten egg and vanilla extract.

3 Sift the flour, baking soda and salt together in another bowl.

4 Gradually add a third of the dry ingredients to the mixture, followed by a third of the buttermilk. Continue adding both alternately and mix well until all of the ingredients are combined to form a thick, smooth cake mixture. Be careful not to overmix.

5 Separate equal measures of the prepared cake mixture into five bowls and add different food colorings to each bowl, mixing well.

6 Transfer the different colored cake mixtures into piping bags (do not cut the end until the bags are filled).

7 Cut the tip of each bag and squeeze out a small amount of colored cake mix into each pie tray compartment. Repeat this process with each color until the pan is full.

8 Bake in the oven for 12–14 minutes until risen and firm to the touch.

9 Cool for 5 minutes in the pans before transferring to a wire rack to cool completely.

Rainbow Buttercream

Extra equipment:
2 small piping bags
1 large piping bag with
a large round tip nozzle

Ingredients:
¾ stick (⅓ cup) unsalted butter
2 cups (9 oz) confectioner's sugar
2 tbsps milk
2 food colorings, any colors

1 Beat the butter and confectioner's sugar together for a few minutes using a whisk or an electric mixer until well mixed.

Top Tip!
Just before you put your whoopie pies in the oven, tap the pan onto a work surface several times to ensure the mixture is as flat as possible before baking.

2 Add the milk and beat together until the buttercream is light and fluffy.

3 Separate the buttercream into two bowls and color with two contrasting rainbow colors.

4 Fill two small piping bags with the different colored buttercream. Then snip the ends of both bags and insert them into the large piping bag.

5 Carefully pipe the buttercream onto one half of the rainbow whoopie, ensuring that both colors are visible.

6 Sandwich together and enjoy!

Raspberry Whoopie Pies
with Raspberry Ripple Cream Cheese Filling

Raspberry Whoopie Pies

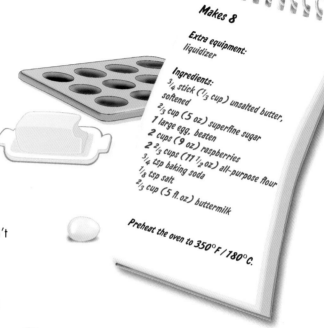

Makes 8

Extra equipment:
liquidizer

Ingredients:
3/4 stick (1/3 cup) unsalted butter, softened
2/3 cup (5 oz) superfine sugar
1 large egg, beaten
2 cups (9 oz) raspberries
2 2/3 cups (11 1/2 oz) all-purpose flour
3/4 tsp baking soda
1/8 tsp salt
2/3 cup (5 fl. oz) buttermilk

Preheat the oven to 350°F/180°C.

1 Grease the whoopie pie pans with a little butter.

2 Cream the softened butter and sugar together in a bowl until light and fluffy, then gradually add the beaten egg.

3 Process half of the raspberries in a liquidizer for several minutes until they have broken down into a liquid. If you don't have a liquidizer, ask an adult to use a hand held mixer.

4 Add to the creamed butter mixture and mix well for a few minutes.

5 Sift the flour, baking soda and salt together in another bowl.

6 Gradually add a third of the dry ingredients to the mixture, followed by a third of the buttermilk. Continue adding both alternately and mix well until all of the ingredients are combined to form a thick, smooth cake mixture.

7 Add the remaining whole raspberries and mix well with a spoon until evenly combined.

8 Fill a piping bag or use a tablespoon to transfer the cake mixture evenly onto the whoopie pie pans.

9 Bake in the oven for 12–14 minutes until risen and firm to the touch.

10 Cool for 5 minutes in the pans before transferring to a wire rack to cool completely.

Raspberry Ripple Cream Cheese Filling

1 Beat the butter and confectioner's sugar together for a few minutes using a whisk or an electric mixer until well mixed.

2 Add the cream cheese and beat together until the filling is light and fluffy.

3 Process the raspberries in a liquidizer and then add the sieved confectioner's sugar and lemon juice. If you haven't got a liquidizer, ask an adult to use a hand held mixer.

4 Pour the raspberry sauce through a sieve into a jug, to remove all of the raspberry seeds.

5 Using a tablespoon, spread the filling onto half of the whoopie pies, drizzle with raspberry sauce and then sandwich together with the remaining halves.

Extra equipment:
liquidizer

Ingredients:
$1/2$ stick ($1/4$ cup) unsalted butter
$2 1/2$ cups (10 $1/2$ oz) confectioner's sugar
$1/2$ cup (4 $1/2$ oz) cream cheese
1 cup (4 $1/2$ oz) raspberries
$1/3$ cup (1 $1/2$ oz) confectioner's sugar, sieved
$1 1/2$ tsps lemon juice

Red Velvet
Whoopie Pies
with Marshmallow Cream Cheese Filling

Red Velvet Whoopie Pies

Makes 8

Ingredients:
3/4 stick (1/3 cup) unsalted butter, softened
3/4 cup (5 oz) light brown sugar
1 large egg, beaten
1 tsp vanilla extract
1 tsp red food coloring
2 1/4 cups (10 oz) all-purpose flour
2 tbsps baking cocoa
2/3 cup (5 fl. oz) buttermilk
3/4 tsp baking soda
3/4 tsp white wine vinegar
1/8 tsp salt

Preheat the oven to 350°F / 180°C.

1 Grease the whoopie pie pans with a little butter.

2 Cream the softened butter and sugar together in a bowl until light and fluffy, then gradually add the beaten egg, vanilla extract and red food coloring, ensuring everything is well mixed.

3 Sift in half of the flour and baking cocoa to the mixture, followed by half of the buttermilk and then repeat until all of the ingredients are combined to form a thick, smooth cake mixture.

4 Add the baking soda, white wine vinegar and salt and continue to mix well for a few minutes.

5 Fill a piping bag or use a tablespoon to transfer the cake mixture onto the whoopie pie pans.

6 Bake in the oven for 12–14 minutes until risen and firm to the touch.

7 Cool for 5 minutes in the pans before transferring to a wire rack to cool completely.

Marshmallow Cream Cheese Filling

1 Beat the butter and cream cheese together. Then, using a spoon dipped in hot water, add the marshmallow creme.

2 Gradually add all of the confectioner's sugar and continue to mix for several minutes, until you are left with a smooth, silky looking filling.

3 Using either a piping bag or a spoon, spread the filling evenly over one half of the whoopie pie and sandwich together with the second half.

Ingredients:
1 stick (½ cup) butter
1 cup (8 oz) cream cheese
1 jar (7 ½ oz) marshmallow creme
3 ²/₃ cups (1 lb) confectioner's sugar

Top Tip!
If the marshmallow filling is too runny, either add more confectioner's sugar or refrigerate for a little while before piping.

Spiced Apple & Cinnamon Whoopie Pies
with Cinnamon Buttercream

Spiced Apple & Cinnamon Whoopie Pies

1 Grease the whoopie pie pans with a little butter.

2 Cream the softened butter and sugar together in a bowl until light and fluffy, then gradually add the beaten egg.

3 Sift in half of the flour, the cinnamon, nutmeg, cloves, baking soda and salt, followed by half of the buttermilk. Repeat until all of the ingredients are combined to form a thick, smooth cake mixture.

4 Stir in the small apple pieces.

5 Fill a piping bag or use a tablespoon to transfer the cake mixture evenly onto the whoopie pie pans.

6 Bake in the oven for 12–14 minutes until risen and firm to the touch.

7 Cool for 5 minutes in the pans before transferring to a wire rack to cool completely.

Makes 8

Ingredients:
3/4 stick (1/3 cup) unsalted butter, softened
3/4 cup (5 oz) light brown sugar
1 large egg, beaten
2 1/4 cups (10 oz) all-purpose flour
1/2 tsp ground cinnamon
1/4 tsp ground nutmeg
1/8 tsp ground cloves
3/4 tsp baking soda
1/8 tsp salt
2/3 cup (5 fl. oz) buttermilk
1 cooking apple, peeled, cored and cut into small pieces

Preheat the oven to 350°F / 180°C.

Cinnamon Buttercream

1 Beat the butter, confectioner's sugar and cinnamon together for a few minutes using a whisk or an electric mixer until well mixed.

2 Add the cream cheese and beat together until the buttercream is light and fluffy.

3 Using either a piping bag or a spoon, spread the buttercream evenly over one half of the whoopie pie and sandwich together with the second half.

Ingredients:
1/2 stick (1/4 cup) unsalted butter
2 1/2 cups (10 1/2 oz) confectioner's sugar
1/8 tsp ground cinnamon
1/2 cup (4 1/2 oz) cream cheese

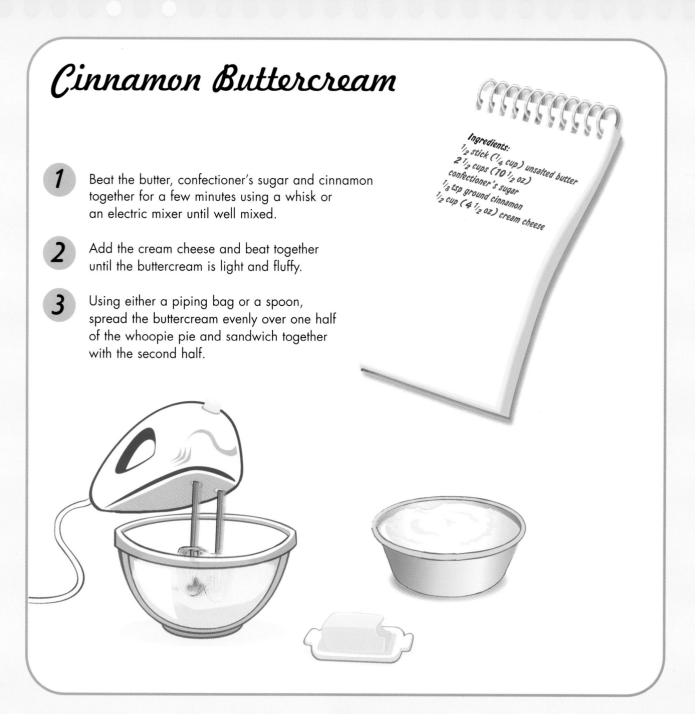

Strawberries & Cream
Whoopie Pies
with Whipped Cream & Fresh Strawberry Filling

Strawberries & Cream Whoopie Pies

Makes 8

Extra equipment:
liquidizer

Ingredients:
3/4 cup (5 oz) strawberries, hulled and halved
3/4 stick (1/3 cup) unsalted butter, softened
3/4 cup (5 oz) light brown sugar
1 large egg, beaten
2 1/4 cups (10 oz) all-purpose flour
3/4 tsp baking soda
1/8 tsp salt
2/3 cup (5 fl. oz) buttermilk

Preheat the oven to 350°F / 180°C.

1 Grease the whoopie pie pans with a little butter.

2 Add the halved strawberries to a liquidizer and carefully pulse for a few seconds until the strawberries have broken down into small pieces. Transfer to a bowl and set to one side. If you haven't got a liquidizer, ask an adult to use a hand held mixer.

3 Cream the softened butter and sugar together in a bowl until light and fluffy, then gradually add the beaten egg.

4 Sift the flour, baking soda and salt together in another bowl.

5 Gradually add a third of the dry ingredients to the mixture, followed by a third of the buttermilk. Continue adding both alternately and mix well until all of the ingredients are combined to form a thick, smooth cake mixture.

6 Fold in the chopped strawberries until they are combined evenly with the cake mixture.

7 Fill a piping bag or use a tablespoon to transfer the cake mixture evenly onto the whoopie pie pans.

8 Bake in the oven for 12–14 minutes until risen and firm to the touch.

9 Cool for 5 minutes in the pans before transferring to a wire rack to cool completely.

Whipped Cream & Fresh Strawberry Filling

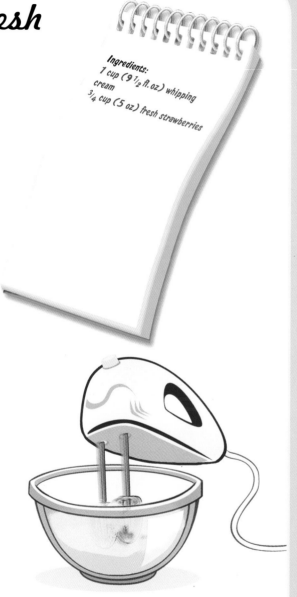

Ingredients:
1 cup (9 ½ fl. oz) whipping cream
¾ cup (5 oz) fresh strawberries

1 Whip the cream using an electric mixer or free-standing mixer until stiff peaks form.

2 Carefully spoon or pipe the cream onto a whoopie pie half.

3 Thinly slice the strawberries and lay them on top of the cream before sandwiching together with another whoopie pie half.

4 Remember to cover the whipped cream and store in the refrigerator if you are not using it straight away.

Vanilla Bean
Whoopie Pies
with Chocolate Buttercream

Vanilla Bean Whoopie Pies

Makes 8

Ingredients:
3/4 stick (1/3 cup) unsalted butter, softened
2/3 cup (5 oz) superfine sugar
1 large egg, beaten
2 1/4 cups (10 oz) all-purpose flour
3/4 tsp baking soda
1/8 tsp salt
2/3 cup (5 fl. oz) buttermilk
1 vanilla bean
(or 1 tsp vanilla extract)

Preheat the oven to 350°F / 180°C.

1 Grease the whoopie pie pans with a little butter.

2 Cream the softened butter and sugar together in a bowl until light and fluffy, then gradually add the beaten egg until well mixed.

3 Sift the flour, baking soda and salt together into another bowl.

4 Gradually add a third of the dry ingredients to the mixture, followed by a third of the buttermilk. Continue adding both alternately and mix well until all of the ingredients are combined to form a thick, smooth cake mixture.

5 Scrape the seeds from the vanilla bean and add to the mixture. Mix for one minute. Alternatively, add 1 teaspoon of vanilla extract.

6 Fill a piping bag or use a tablespoon to transfer the cake mixture evenly onto the whoopie pie pans.

7 Bake in the oven for 12–14 minutes until risen and firm to the touch.

8 Cool for 5 minutes in the pans before transferring to a wire rack to cool completely.

Chocolate Buttercream

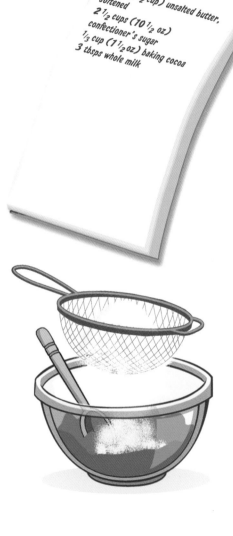

Ingredients:
1 stick (¹/₂ cup) unsalted butter, softened
2 ¹/₂ cups (10 ¹/₂ oz) confectioner's sugar
¹/₃ cup (1 ¹/₂ oz) baking cocoa
3 tbsps whole milk

1 Beat the butter, confectioner's sugar and baking cocoa together for a few minutes using a whisk or an electric mixer until well mixed.

2 Add the milk and mix well for several minutes until the buttercream is light and fluffy.

3 Using either a piping bag or a spoon, spread the buttercream evenly over one half of the whoopie pie and sandwich together with the second half.

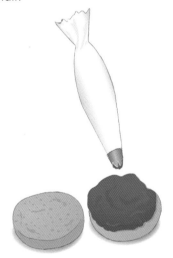

White Chocolate & Marshmallow Whoopie Pies
with White Chocolate Marshmallow Filling

White Chocolate & Marshmallow Whoopie Pies

1 Grease the whoopie pie pans with a little butter.

2 Cream the softened butter and sugar together in a bowl until light and fluffy, then gradually add the beaten egg until well mixed.

3 Sift the flour, baking soda and salt together into another bowl.

4 Gradually add a third of the dry ingredients to the mixture, followed by a third of the buttermilk. Continue adding both alternately and mix well until all of the ingredients are combined to form a thick, smooth cake mixture.

5 Add the broken pieces of white chocolate and stir until evenly combined.

6 Fill a piping bag or use a tablespoon to transfer the cake mixture evenly onto the whoopie pie pans.

7 Bake in the oven for 12–14 minutes until risen and firm to the touch.

8 Cool for 5 minutes in the pans before transferring to a wire rack to cool completely.

Makes 8

Ingredients:
3/4 stick (1/3 cup) unsalted butter, softened
2/3 cup (5 oz) superfine sugar
1 large egg, beaten
2 1/4 cups (10 oz) all-purpose flour
1 1/2 tsps baking soda
1/8 tsp salt
2/3 cup (5 fl. oz) buttermilk
3 1/2 oz white chocolate, broken into small pieces

Preheat the oven to 350°F / 180°C.

White Chocolate Marshmallow Filling

Ingredients:
4 oz white chocolate
1 jar (7 ½ oz) marshmallow creme

1 Break the chocolate into small pieces and carefully melt the chocolate in a microwave, stirring at 30 second intervals. Alternatively, melt the chocolate in a bowl over a saucepan of simmering water, making sure the bowl doesn't touch the water.

2 Add the melted chocolate to the marshmallow creme and mix well.

3 Spread the filling evenly over one half of the whoopie pie and sandwich together with the remaining halves.

Top Tip!
These whoopie pies need to be served straight away as the filling will run out of the whoopie pies easily.

Cake Pops

It's easy to make lots of different cake pops! Once you have mastered the basic cake balls, there is no end to the decorations you can try! Each of the recipes include step-by-step instructions on how to decorate your cake pops. Any extra equipment or ingredients needed to decorate the pops are listed at the beginning of each recipe.

Basic Cake Recipe

Cake balls are bite-sized balls of crumbled cake, mixed with frosting. This recipe, which is enough to make 20, can be used as a basis for your cake pops, or use store-bought cake and frosting instead.

1 Cream the butter and sugar together until pale and fluffy. Add the vanilla extract and mix in.

2 Add the eggs, one at a time, mixing well. Add half of the flour and half of the milk and mix until well combined. Repeat with the remaining flour and milk.

3 Pour the mixture into the pan and bake for 35–45 minutes, or until cooked through. Leave to cool completely on a wire rack.

4 For the frosting, cream the butter and cream cheese together.

5 Gradually add the confectioner's sugar and beat until light and fluffy. Add the vanilla extract. Refrigerate for 30 minutes before using.

Extra equipment:
10 in. (25 cm) round cake pan or
8 in. (20 cm) square cake pan

Ingredients:
1 stick (4 oz) unsalted butter, softened
3/4 cup (5 oz) superfine sugar
1 tsp vanilla extract
2 eggs
1 1/2 cups (6 oz) self-rising flour
4 tbsps milk
For the frosting:
3/4 stick (1/3 cup) unsalted butter, softened
1/4 cup (1 1/2 oz) cream cheese, softened
1 2/3 cups (7 oz) confectioner's sugar, sifted
1 tsp vanilla extract

Preheat the oven to 350°F / 180°C.

Cake Pop Mixture

1 Line a baking sheet with wax paper.

2 Break the cake into small crumbs using your fingers or a liquidizer.

3 Add the frosting into the crumbled cake mixture. Mix with your hands until you are left with a moist mixture that can be easily molded.

4 Weigh out $1/4$ cup (1 oz) portions of cake mixture and mold into shape.

5 Place the pops in the freezer for 10 minutes to harden before decorating.

Extra equipment:
baking sheet
wax paper
liquidizer (optional)

Ingredients:
pre-made cake
pre-made frosting

Cake Pop Equipment

Cake pops are inserted onto lollipop sticks so they are easy to eat and display. Lollipop sticks can be bought from supermarkets, specialist baking stores or online. Styrofoam blocks are great for holding and displaying your pops—don't forget to poke the sticks through first to make holes!

The cake pop decorations in this book include some more specialist baking ingredients—if you can't find them in supermarkets or baking stores, try to think up alternative decorations to make the pops your own!

Dice
Cake Pops

These dotty dice cake pops are the tastiest treats on a stick!

Dice Cake Pops

Extra equipment:
lollipop sticks
styrofoam blocks

Ingredients:
14 oz (400 g) white candy coating
1–2 tbsps vegetable oil
black gum paste
edible glue

1 See pages 71–72 for the basic cake pop recipe—you will need cube shapes for these dice pops.

2 Place the white candy coating in a microwaveable bowl and heat in a microwave at 30 second intervals until they are completely melted.

3 Add 1–2 tablespoons of vegetable oil to thin the coating and stir well.

4 Dip ¹/₂ in. (1 cm) of the lollipop sticks into the candy coating and insert into the bottom of the dice pops. Leave to stand in the styrofoam block.

5 Dip the dice pops carefully into the melted candy until completely covered.

6 Carefully shake off any excess candy coating and place back in the styrofoam block until completely dry.

7 Ask an adult to cut out enough circles from black gum paste to assemble as the dots on the dice.

8 When completely dry, attach the dots to the dice pops with a small amount of edible glue.

Top Tip!
The ingredient quantities on pages 71–72 are for **20** cake pops. If you want to make more or less, adjust the ingredients accordingly!

Mushroom Cake Pops

A spotty pop to enjoy any time of the day!

Mushroom Cake Pops

1 See pages 71–72 for the basic cake pop recipe—you will need to split the 1/4 cup (1 oz) portions of mixture into equal portions, both 1/8 cup (1/2 oz).

2 Mold the first portions into the cylinder-shaped stalk of the mushroom and place on wax paper.

3 Roll the remaining portions into balls and flatten in the palm of your hand to form the mushroom caps.

4 Place the white candy coating in a microwaveable bowl and heat in a microwave at 30 second intervals until they are completely melted.

5 Add 1–2 tablespoons of vegetable oil to thin the coating and stir well.

6 Using a paintbrush, apply a small amount of candy coating onto the top of the mushroom stalks and attach the caps.

7 Place the mushroom pops in a freezer for 10 minutes to cool.

8 Dip 1/2 in. (1 cm) of the lollipop sticks into the candy coating and insert into the bottom of the mushroom pops.

Extra equipment:
wax paper
lollipop sticks
styrofoam blocks
paintbrush

Ingredients:
14 oz white candy coating
1–2 tbsps vegetable oil
14 oz red candy coating

9 After a few minutes, dip the mushroom pops carefully into the melted candy until completely covered.

10 Stand in a styrofoam block to dry for a few minutes.

11 Melt the red candy coating as before and dip the top half of the mushroom pops into the melted candy.

12 Once completely dry, use a paintbrush to add white spots to the mushroom tops using melted white candy.

Ghost Cake Pops

These spooky ghost cake pops are perfect for Halloween!

Ghost Cake Pops

1 See pages 71–72 for the basic cake pop recipe—you will need round balls for these ghost pops.

2 Melt the black candy coating in a microwaveable bowl and heat in a microwave at 30 second intervals until they are completely melted.

3 Add 1–2 tablespoons of vegetable oil to thin the coating and stir well.

4 Dip $1/2$ in. (1 cm) of the lollipop sticks into the candy coating and insert into the bottom of the pops. Leave to stand in a styrofoam block.

5 Roll out a piece of white fondant to approximately $1/4$ in. (5 mm) thickness.

6 Ask an adult to cut out a rough circular shape, large enough to cover the cake pop. Then, cut out two eyes and a mouth from the frosting.

7 Brush a little melted candy onto the top of the cake pop before placing the ghost "sheet" over the cake pop.

Extra equipment:
lollipop sticks
styrofoam blocks
paintbrush

Ingredients:
14 oz black candy coating
1–2 tbsps vegetable oil
white ready-to-roll fondant

Gift
Cake Pops
Transform these pops into colorful gifts!

Gift Cake Pops

1 See pages 71–72 for the basic cake pop recipe—you will need cube shapes for these gift pops.

2 Place the colored candy coating in microwaveable bowl and heat in a microwave at 30 second intervals until they are completely melted.

3 Add 1–2 tablespoons of vegetable oil to thin the coating and stir well.

4 Dip $1/2$ in. (1 cm) of the lollipop sticks into the candy coating and insert into the bottom of the gift pops. Leave to stand in a styrofoam block.

5 Dip the gift pops carefully into the melted candy until completely covered.

6 Carefully shake off any excess candy coating and place back in the styrofoam block to dry completely.

7 Roll out a thin piece of colored modeling paste and ask an adult to cut into long strips using a craft knife.

8 Brush the underside of the strips with a small amount of edible glue and lay them around the gift pops to form ribbons.

Extra equipment:
lollipop sticks
styrofoam blocks
shaped silicone mold

Ingredients:
14 oz candy coating (any color)
1–2 tbsps vegetable oil
colored modeling paste
edible glue

Top Tip!
If you can't find a small silicone mold, ask an adult to cut out a pretty shape with a sharp knife.

9 Press a small amount of modeling paste into a tiny shaped silicone mold, carefully removing any excess. Remove the shape from the mold and glue to the top of the gift pop. Repeat for the remaining pops.

10 Repeat with different colored candy coating for a selection of colorful gift pops!

Flower Cake Pops

These beautiful flower cake pops will brighten up any room!

Flower Cake Pops

1 See pages 71–72 for the basic cake pop recipe—you will need tulip shapes for these flower pops.

2 Place the colored candy coating in a microwaveable bowl and heat in a microwave at 30 second intervals until they are completely melted.

3 Add 1–2 tablespoons of vegetable oil to thin the coating and stir well.

4 Dip $1/2$ in. (1 cm) of the lollipop sticks into the candy coating and insert into the bottom of the pops. Leave to stand in a styrofoam block.

5 Dip the pops carefully into the melted candy until completely covered.

6 Carefully shake off any excess candy coating and place back in the styrofoam block to dry.

7 Roll out a piece of modeling paste and, using a craft knife, ask an adult to cut out four petals, ensuring that they are taller than the cake pop.

8 Using melted candy as glue, attach each petal to the side of the flower pop and leave to dry.

9 Repeat with different colored modeling paste for a selection of colorful flowers!

Extra equipment:
lollipop sticks
styrofoam blocks
craft knife

Ingredients:
14 oz candy coating (any color)
1–2 tbsps vegetable oil
modeling paste

Pig
Cake Pops

Oink! Oink! These little piggies are too cute to eat!

Pig Cake Pops

Extra equipment:
lollipop sticks
styrofoam blocks

Ingredients:
pink gum paste
white gum paste
black candy writer
14 oz pink candy coating
1–2 tbsps vegetable oil
pink luster dust

Top Tip!
If you can't find luster dust, look out for shimmer spray in supermarkets.

1 Hand model two pig's ears from pink gum paste. Once you are happy with their shape, place the ears around a lollipop stick to bend the ears into shape.

2 Now model a pig's snout from the paste, using the end of a lollipop stick to create the nostrils.

3 Ask an adult to cut out two small circles for eyes from white gum paste. Repeat making two ears, a snout and two eyes for each cake pop.

4 Using a candy writer, carefully paint on the black centers of the eyes and leave to dry.

5 See pages 71–72 for the basic cake pop recipe —you will need round balls for these pig pops.

6 Place the pink candy coating in a microwaveable bowl and heat in a microwave at 30 second intervals until they are completely melted.

7 Add 1–2 tablespoons of vegetable oil to thin the coating and stir well.

8 Dip 1/2 in. (1 cm) of the lollipop sticks into the candy coating and insert into the bottom of the pig pops. Leave to stand in a styrofoam block.

9 Dip the pops carefully into the melted candy until completely covered.

10 Carefully shake off any excess candy coating and, while still wet, attach the prepared snout, eyes and ears.

11 Place back in the styrofoam block to dry.

12 Using a small paintbrush, apply pink luster dust to enhance cheek areas.

Christmas Cake Pops

These festive pops make fantastic gifts for family and friends!

Christmas Cake Pops

1. Ask an adult to cut out two holly leaves from green gum paste and two small berries from red gum paste. Set aside.

2. See pages 71–72 for the basic cake pop recipe—you will need round balls with flattened bases. Use a work surface to carefully flatten the base of each pop.

3. Place the dark chocolate candy coating in a microwaveable bowl and heat in a microwave at 30 second intervals until they are completely melted.

4. Add 1–2 tablespoons of vegetable oil to thin the coating and stir well.

5. Dip $1/2$ in. (1 cm) of the lollipop sticks into the candy coating and insert into the bottom of the pop. Leave to stand in a styrofoam block.

6. Dip the pops carefully into the melted candy until completely covered.

7. Carefully shake off any excess candy coating and place back in the styrofoam block to dry.

8. When the pops are completely dry, use the white candy writer to create the effect of cake frosting onto the top of each cake pop.

9. Using a small amount of edible glue, attach the holly leaves and berries on top of the Christmas pudding pops.

10. Try topping each of your Christmas pops with different festive-themed decorations.

Extra equipment:
lollipop sticks
styrofoam blocks

Ingredients:
green gum paste
red gum paste
14 oz dark chocolate candy coating
1–2 tbsps vegetable oil
white candy writer
edible glue

Top Tip!
Sprinkle with a dusting of confectioner's sugar to finish!

Star
Cake Pops

You'll be a star with your friends when you give them these star cake pops!

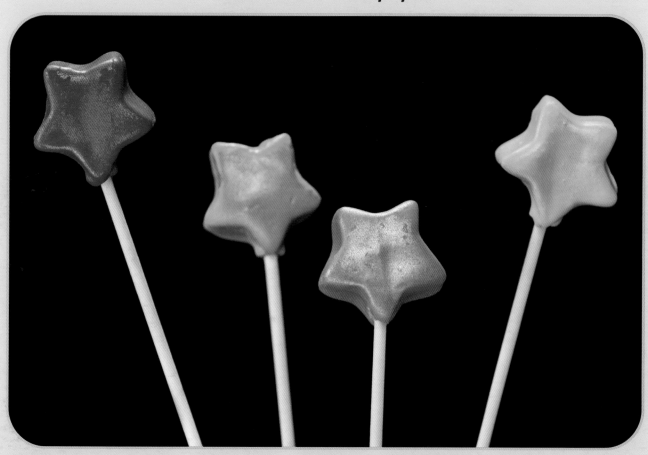

Star Cake Pops

Extra equipment:
star cutter
lollipop sticks
styrofoam blocks
fine paintbrush

Ingredients:
14 oz candy coating (any color)
1–2 tbsps vegetable oil
edible luster dust

1 See pages 71–72 for the basic cake pop recipe—you will need to use a star cutter to make star shapes for these pops.

2 Place the colored candy coating in a microwaveable bowl and heat in a microwave at 30 second intervals until they are completely melted.

3 Add 1–2 tablespoons of vegetable oil to thin the coating and stir well.

4 Dip 1/2 in. (1 cm) of the lollipop sticks into the candy coating and insert into the bottom of the star pops. Leave to stand in a styrofoam block.

5 Dip the star pops carefully into the melted candy until completely covered.

6 Carefully shake off any excess candy coating and place back in the styrofoam block to dry completely.

7 Using a fine paintbrush, apply different colored edible luster dust to the stars to create a shimmer effect.

8 Repeat with different colored candy coating for a selection of colorful stars!

Heart
Cake Pops

Give your Valentine a gift to remember with these lovable pops!

Heart Cake Pops

1 See pages 71–72 for the basic cake pop recipe—you will need heart shapes for these pops.

2 Place the pink candy coating in a microwaveable bowl and heat in a microwave at 30 second intervals until they are completely melted.

3 Press a small amount of modeling paste into a tiny bow-shaped silicone mold, carefully removing any excess, and pop out onto wax paper. If you haven't got a mold, ask an adult to cut out shapes using a sharp knife.

4 Dip $1/2$ in. (1 cm) of the lollipop sticks into the candy coating and insert into the bottom of the heart cake pops. Leave to stand in the styrofoam block.

5 Add 1–2 tablespoons of vegetable oil to thin the coating and stir well.

6 Carefully dip the heart pops into the melted candy and turn slowly until completely coated. Gently shake to remove any excess and avoid dripping.

Extra equipment:
bow-shaped silicone mold
wax paper
lollipop sticks
styrofoam blocks

Ingredients:
14 oz pink candy coating
modeling paste
1–2 tbsps vegetable oil
pink sanding sugar

Top Tip!
If you can't find a styrofoam block, look for cardboard or foam stands to hold your cake pops.

7 Sprinkle pink sanding sugar over the wet candy and hold the modeled bow into position until the candy dries.

8 Place back in the styrofoam block until completely dry.

Strawberry
Cake Pops

These super strawberry pops make a great summer treat!

Strawberry Cake Pops

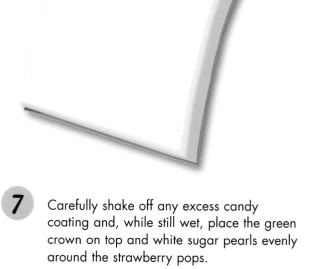

Extra equipment:
small flower cutter
lollipop sticks
styrofoam blocks

Ingredients:
green gum paste
14 oz red candy coating
1–2 tbsps vegetable oil
white sugar pearls

1 Using a small flower cutter, cut out the crown of the strawberry from green gum paste and put to one side. Alternatively, ask an adult to cut out the shape with a sharp knife.

2 See pages 71–72 for the basic cake pop recipe—you will need strawberry shapes for these pops.

3 Place the red candy coating in a microwaveable bowl and heat in a microwave at 30 second intervals until they are completely melted.

4 Add 1–2 tablespoons of vegetable oil to thin the coating and stir well.

5 Dip $^1/_2$ in. (1 cm) of the lollipop sticks into the candy coating and insert into the bottom of the strawberry pops. Leave to stand in a styrofoam block.

6 Dip the strawberry pops carefully into the melted candy until completely covered.

7 Carefully shake off any excess candy coating and, while still wet, place the green crown on top and white sugar pearls evenly around the strawberry pops.

8 Place back in the styrofoam block to dry completely.

Frog
Cake Pops

Ribbit! Ribbit! These cheerful pops are frog-tastic!

Frog Cake Pops

1 See pages 71–72 for the basic cake pop recipe—you will need round balls for these pops.

2 Roll two small balls for the eyes from the cake mixture and attach to the top of the frog pops with melted candy coating.

3 Place the cake pops back in a freezer for 10 minutes to harden.

4 Place the green candy coating in a microwaveable bowl and heat in a microwave at 30 second intervals until they are completely melted.

5 Add 1–2 tablespoons of vegetable oil to thin the coating and stir well.

6 Dip 1/2 in. (1 cm) of the lollipop sticks into the candy coating and insert into the bottom of the frog pops. Leave to stand in a styrofoam block.

7 Dip the pops carefully into the melted candy until completely covered.

8 Carefully shake off any excess candy coating and place back in the styrofoam block to dry.

9 Ask an adult to cut out small half circles from white gum paste and attach small pieces of black gum paste to form the frogs' eyes.

10 When the frog pops are completely dry, attach the eyes using edible glue.

11 Using a black candy writer, carefully draw on the frogs' mouths and leave to dry. Try giving each frog a different expression to make each Frog Pop individual.

12 The method to create "eyes" can be used to make other animal-inspired pops.

Extra equipment:
lollipop sticks
styrofoam blocks

Ingredients:
14 oz green candy coating
1–2 tbsps vegetable oil
white gum paste
black gum paste
edible glue
black candy writer

Top Tip!
Make sure your bowl is about 3 in. (8 cm) full with melted candy so the cake pops don't touch the sides or bottom of the bowl when dipped.

Cupcake Cake Pops

Everyone loves a cupcake and they'll love them even more
in the form of these pops!

Cupcake Cake Pops

1 Press a small amount of pink modeling paste into a rose-shaped silicone mold and pop out onto wax paper. Alternatively, ask an adult to cut out a similar shape with a sharp knife.

2 See pages 71–72 for the basic cake pop recipe.

3 Weigh out 1/4 cup (1 oz) portions of cake mixture and press into a cupcake-shaped cake pop mold. Alternatively, divide the cake mixture into two portions, one slightly larger than the other. Mold the larger portion into the cylinder-shaped cupcake base. Roll the smaller piece into a ball and flatten to form the top of the cupcake.

4 Attach the two cake pieces together using melted candy coating and leave to dry for a few minutes.

5 Place the cupcake pops in a freezer for 10 minutes to harden.

6 Place the dark chocolate candy coating in a microwaveable bowl and heat in a microwave at 30 second intervals until they are completely melted.

7 Add 1–2 tablespoons of vegetable oil to thin the coating and stir well.

Extra equipment:
rose-shaped silicone mold (optional)
wax paper
cupcake-shaped cake pop mold
lollipop sticks
styrofoam blocks

Ingredients:
pink modeling paste
14 oz dark chocolate candy coating
1–2 tbsps vegetable oil
7 oz pink candy coating
candy sprinkles

Top Tip!
You can dip the entire cupcake into the first candy coating instead of using the two-step method!

8 Dip 1/2 in. (1 cm) of the lollipop sticks into the candy coating and insert into the bottom of the cupcake pops. Leave to stand in a styrofoam block.

9 Dip the cupcake pops into the melted candy until completely covered.

10 Carefully shake off any excess candy coating and place back in the styrofoam block to dry.

11 Repeat the melting process with pink candy coating. When the pops are dry, carefully dip the top of the cupcake into the melted pink candy.

12 Before the pops are dry, add candy sprinkles to the top and place the prepared rose or other small decorations to finish.